The Wee Adventures of Shabu Shabu™

A thrilling tale told in eight parts

Book 1
The Jade Legend

By Michael Csokas and Kristina Thornton

Copyright 2013
Steam Powered Productions

  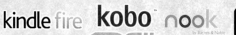 

www.shabusworld.com   www.facebook.com/theweeadventuresofshabushabu

To all our family and friends,
wherever in time and space
you may be.

THE WEE ADVENTURES OF SHABU SHABU™ – BOOK 1 – THE JADE LEGEND

Copyright © 2013 by Steam Powered Productions Pte Ltd
ISBN: 978-981-07-5976-6

Steam Powered Productions Pte Ltd
info@shabusworld.com
www.shabusworld.com
www.facebook.com/TheWeeAdventuresofShabuShabu

"Grandfather, look! So many stars!"

"Yes, my little Shabu Shabu, so many stars. Would you like to see them up close?"

From inside his oil-stained apron, Grandfather pulled out a tiny handmade brass spyglass and put it into the baby rabbit's eager paws. He then sat down and lifted the little rabbit onto his lap.

"Do you remember what those stars are called?" Grandfather asked as he stretched out a paw towards the sky.

Shabu peered through the spyglass.

"The con-suh-lay-shun of the Peacock's Treasure?"

"Very good. And that one?" He lowered his paw slightly.

"That's the Pouncing Tiger."

"Yes. And that one?"

"That's the Moon, Grandfather!"

"Yes, at its biggest and brightest. I can't fool you, can I? And this time of year we call it the Jade Moon. Do you remember the story of the Jade Legend?"

"Grandfather, you've told me a million times. Of course I remember." She paused.

"Can you tell me again?"

The old rabbit chuckled and stroked her small ear. He reached once again into his apron pocket and withdrew a well-worn scroll. He unfurled it carefully with his calloused paws, and held it up for Shabu to see.

"Once upon a time..."

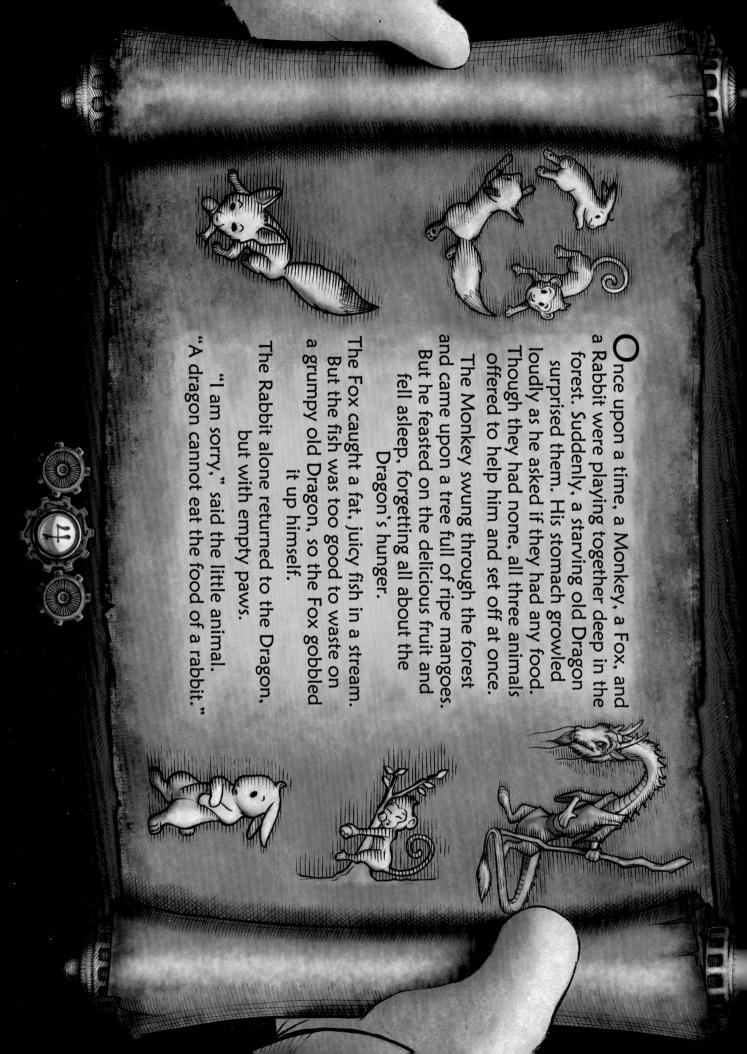

Once upon a time, a Monkey, a Fox, and a Rabbit were playing together deep in the forest. Suddenly, a starving old Dragon surprised them. His stomach growled loudly as he asked if they had any food. Though they had none, all three animals offered to help him and set off at once.

The Monkey swung through the forest and came upon a tree full of ripe mangoes. But he feasted on the delicious fruit and fell asleep, forgetting all about the Dragon's hunger.

The Fox caught a fat, juicy fish in a stream. But the fish was too good to waste on a grumpy old Dragon, so the Fox gobbled it up himself.

The Rabbit alone returned to the Dragon, but with empty paws.

"I am sorry," said the little animal. "A dragon cannot eat the food of a rabbit."

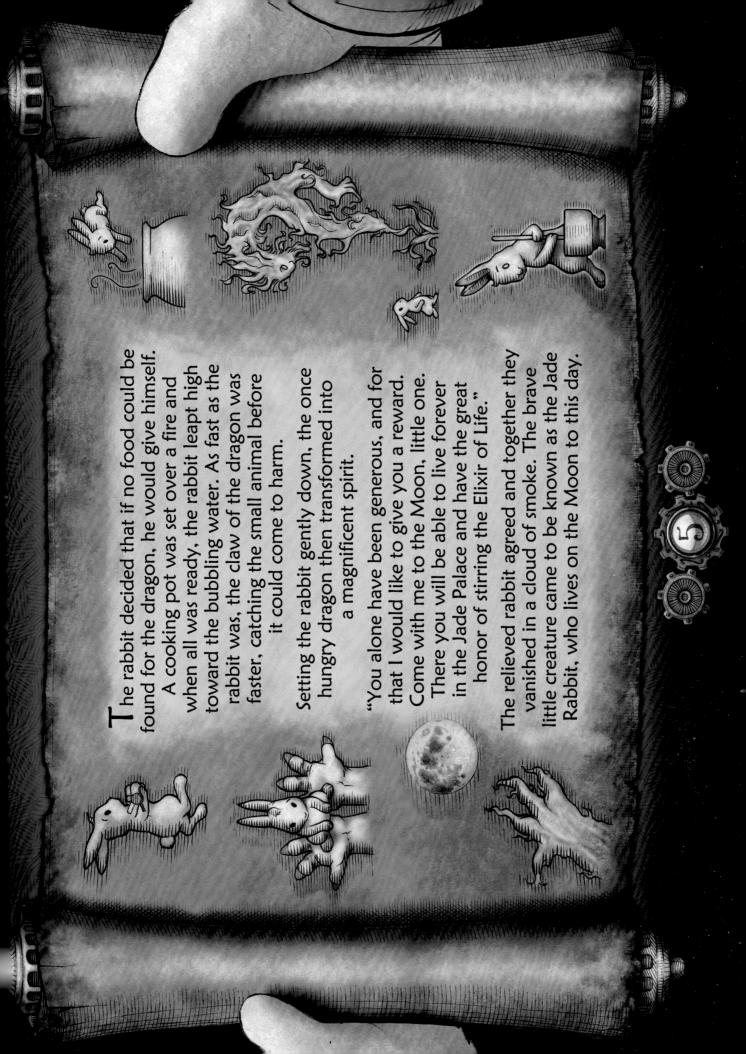

The rabbit decided that if no food could be found for the dragon, he would give himself. A cooking pot was set over a fire and when all was ready, the rabbit leapt high toward the bubbling water. As fast as the rabbit was, the claw of the dragon was faster, catching the small animal before it could come to harm.

Setting the rabbit gently down, the once hungry dragon then transformed into a magnificent spirit.

"You alone have been generous, and for that I would like to give you a reward. Come with me to the Moon, little one. There you will be able to live forever in the Jade Palace and have the great honor of stirring the Elixir of Life."

The relieved rabbit agreed and together they vanished in a cloud of smoke. The brave little creature came to be known as the Jade Rabbit, who lives on the Moon to this day.

"**I**s the Jade Rabbit really up there, Grandfather? I wish I could fly so high, all the way to the Moon and meet him."

"That is just what your father used to say."

"Daddy wanted to meet him too?"

"Shu Shu, your father was as curious about the Moon as you are." Grandfather sighed.

"My heart tells me the Jade Rabbit is up there, watching us. And one day, after much hard work, if you are good and kind, and clever and brave, you just might meet him for yourself."

"Let's build a te-le-le-scope and look for him!"

"A telescope? What a great idea! We can finish one by this time next year. But it may take many years and many telescopes until we're able to peer deep into the secrets of the Moon."

The little rabbit twitched her nose and put her paws on her hips as she looked up at him.

"But I want to find the Jade Rabbit now!"

Grandfather smiled and tapped her on the nose.

"You must also be patient! Speaking of patience..." His own nose twitched as a rich aroma drifted toward them from the burrow.

"I believe we've been up here long enough for dinner to be ready. Shall we go inside and see?"

"Let's go!" shouted Shabu as she leapt from her grandfather's soft lap and hopped through the grass to their burrow. She stood as tall as she could as Grandfather came up beside her. Paw in paw, they made their way down the stone path to their home under the hill.

Shabu Shabu woke in the morning to find Grandfather whistling cheerfully in his lab. He was packing his Inflatable Venture Vessel full of gadgets and goodies.

"Good morning, sleepy-head! You're just in time to help me load this latest Fisheroo onto the balloon."

"Another fishing machine, Grandfather?"

"Yes, their last one slipped off an iceberg. Those Wallowing Walruses have got to be more careful or next time they really might die of laziness."

"Can I come with you? Please?"

"One of these days, my dear. You're much too young yet for such adventures as navigating windy skies and pacifying hungry carnivores. For now, keep to the safety of the burrow and keep your naughty friend Chow out of trouble."

When all was packed
and ready, Grandfather
kissed Shabu's furry cheek
and gave her a giant hug.
Shabu watched him longingly
as he fired up the Venture
Vessel's burner and soared off
into the endless blue sky.

was time to
ok for Chow.

9

Shabu found Chow in their treehouse.

"**W**hat shall we build today, Captain Fuzzy Brain?" asked Chow.

"Well, Captain Noodle Head, we could play with Grandfather's Flammable Flapping Fingamajig."

"Um, it's been broken ever since you tried to give haircuts to the Meany Weeny Kiwi Birds."

"In that case, we could work on my Bellowed Blowhorn!"

"Uh, you do remember what happened last time, don't you?"

"Aw, come on. Don't be such a scaredy squirrel. What could go wrong?"

10

On the far side of the burrow, a trembling machine chugged and thumped and poured out thick clouds of billowing steam.

"It's not working! Turn the bellows to full power!" yelled Shabu over the noise.

"I can't Cap'n! It's too much already!"

"Just a little more…"

"The —wrench—is—stuck!"

Before Shabu could help her friend, Chow's wrench twisted and slipped. A mighty wave of sound and wind blasted from the Bellowed Blowhorn

—BURRRAAAAH!—

sweeping the wee inventors into the air.

11

Clunk! Plunk! Thump!

Shabu Shabu thudded to the ground, and pieces of the Bellowed Blowhown rained down around her. Her ears were ringing. There was no sign of Chow.

"WHAT IS ALL THAT RACKET?" hollered Chow's mother, stepping out from the burrow.

"What about my jacket?" said a small voice from the tire swing.

Shabu stumbled over and pulled Chow to his feet.

"Next time, *I'll* use the wrench," she said.

"Good idea! We *should* build a bench," Chow replied as they wobbled down the path.

Weeks later, while the two friends were playing pirates in the tree house, Shabu spotted Grandfather's balloon on the horizon. They bolted down the stairs, across the yard, and around the corner to the landing dock.

"Careful now," the returning adventurer called as he guided the Venture Vessel downward. The moment the balloon came to a standstill, Shabu and Chow tumbled over the side of the basket and into the arms of the old rabbit.

Grandfather gave them a big squeeze, and then set them down. Shabu looked up and asked,

"What have you brought home this time, Grandfather?"

The old rabbit cleared his throat and reached into a sack hanging over the balloon's basket.

"From the farthest reaches of the frozen north, I give you... Walrus-Whiskered Wizzy Wigs!"

He plopped two hairy hats onto their heads.

"You'll have to write those Wallowing Walruses a thank you note. But first let's go to the lab."

"Now, my little dumplings, what have you been up to while I was away?" Shabu glanced at Chow, and then looked up innocently at Grandfather.

"Oh nothing. Just...playing." Chow gave a small cough from behind his friend.

"Hmm. Where has that Flapping Fingamajig disappeared to? I was thinking of asking young Chow to finish the engine for me..."

Chow dropped the hammer he had been holding. He stood tall and saluted.

"Sir, yes, sir!" he cried, before darting off to find the wreck.

15

"I have something to show you, Shabu."

The old adventurer hopped over to his rucksack and pulled out a second bundle. Shabu lifted out a round piece of glass.

"What's this, Grandfather?"

"This, Shu Shu, is Glacier Glass. Millions of years of natural polishing have made it a remarkable substance that's perfect for magnification—"

"We can use it for our telescope!" interrupted Shabu.

"Yes, but we must hurry. Remember, the Jade Moon only comes once a year and we're running out of time."

Shabu Shabu slipped on her trusty goggles and grinned.

"What are we waiting for?"

16

"Shu Shu, you go first. Tell me what you see."

The little rabbit buried her face in the telescope and gasped.

"I can't see anything, Grandfather!"

"Open your other eye."

"Oh. Ooooo. So many stars, Grandfather! And they're bigger than ever!"

"And the Moon?"

The old rabbit helped Shabu turn the telescope until she could see the dusty gray Moon through the lens.

"I see it, Grandfather, I see it!"

"What do you see? Describe it to me!"

"It's white and gray, and there are big holes, but it's too far away to see much more."

"Too far away? Let me see." Grandfather shook his head.

"This is good work, Shu Shu, but we're going to have to do much better if we want to see any sign of the Jade Rabbit." Shabu sighed.

"I don't think we'll ever see him, Grandfather."

"Cheer up, my dear. A true inventor never gives up but instead seeks a better solution. The next Jade Moon is a year away and we'll be able to build a stronger telescope by then."

"You never stay home long enough, Grandfather," said Shabu. Soon after the annual Jade Moon had passed, he packed his balloon and set off again. Shabu had begged him to let her join him, but again Grandfather refused.

"I'm sorry, Shu Shu, but the world is a dangerous place."

Shabu stood with Chow on top of the burrow and watched the balloon fade to a tiny black speck against the brilliant white clouds.

A few hours later she tried to follow in her Wind-Guided Hover Tub but unfortunately was still missing a few key pieces.

"It's ok, Cap, you'll get to go one of these days," said Chow. He brought her some ice cream and a blowtorch to make her feel better.

Grandfather's answer was always the same after each request. By the time they'd made their fifth telescope together, Shabu Shabu was getting desperate to join Grandfather on his adventures.

"Shu Shu, outside of this burrow, the world is full of mysterious mysteries and dangerous discoveries, vile villains and heroic heroes, booby-trapped treasures and harrowing hardships. You're much safer here at home."

"If Mother and Father were here, they would let me go." Tears welled up in Grandfather's eyes.

"I can't protect you forever, little dumpling, but until you are ready, you will be kept out of harm's way."

"But, Grandfather—"

"That's enough. Now pass me that wrench."

"Why are we building all these telescopes? We're never going to see the Jade Rabbit. He probably doesn't even exist. It's all just a story."

"I suspect one day you will think otherwise. And when that day comes, the winds of adventure will whisk you far away from home. Just don't forget your parachute."

Time passed.

Shabu stood alone in Grandfather's lab, poring over their notes and running her paws over his beloved inventions. Tears flowed down her furry cheek, and she kicked at the loose cobblestone that he had never had time to fix.

With Grandfather gone and Chow's mother looking after his nieces and nephews in a distant tree hollow, the once-bustling burrow was now cold and empty.

"I wish you were still here, Grandfather."

Shabu faced the Lunar Chronometer on the wall. The Jade Moon was quickly approaching.

"It's time to complete Grandfather's final telescope, the biggest and grandest of all."

Days later, Shabu paced the lab as the Moon began to rise. She could hear Chow in another room, tinkering on one of his hare-brained machines.

"What's this?" said Shabu, spying an ornate chest tucked away on a shelf. She opened it and found the miniature brass spyglass Grandfather had given to her so long ago.

She held it up to one eye and stared through the window at the darkening sky.

"There's a storm coming. I'd better hurry."

She carefully set the spyglass on Grandfather's oil-stained desk and pulled a lever on the wall of the underground laboratory.

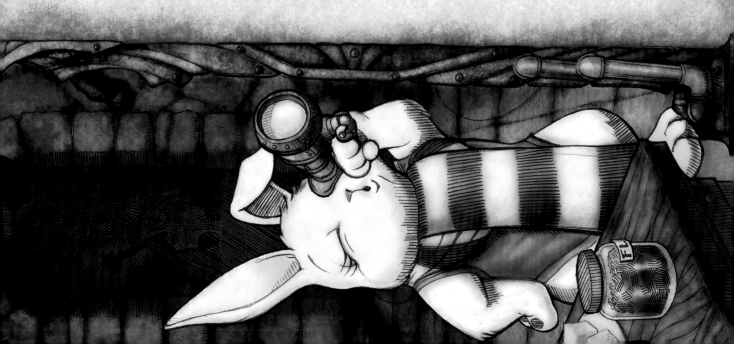

With a loud, grinding noise, a panel in the wall slid upwards and the huge telescope wheeled forward on a platform that extended into the blackness beyond.

Shabu stepped into the night air.

She tilted the giant lens up toward the full Moon and peeked through the eye-piece.

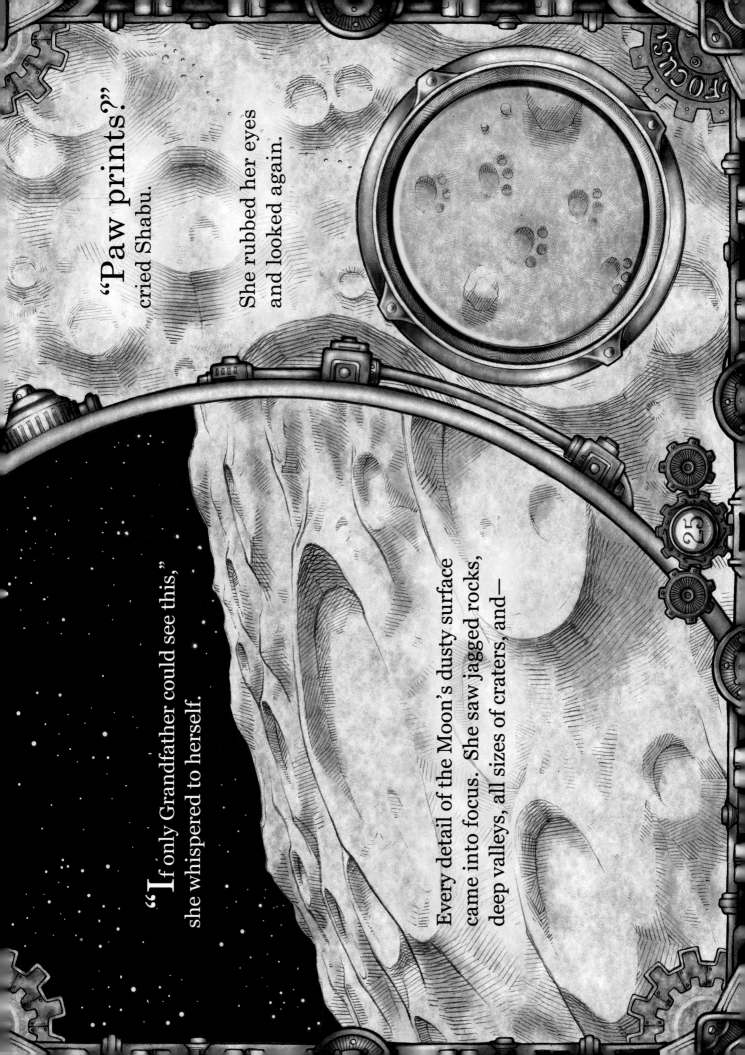

"Paw prints?"
cried Shabu.

She rubbed her eyes
and looked again.

"If only Grandfather could see this,"
she whispered to herself.

Every detail of the Moon's dusty surface
came into focus. She saw jagged rocks,
deep valleys, all sizes of craters, and—

T he prints in the dust were still there.

"But it's just a story!" Shabu followed the path and saw a bright green tail, bright green fur, and a bright green eye peering through a shiny telescope straight back at her.

Shabu held her breath as the bright green rabbit stepped back from his telescope and waved both paws.

She turned a few knobs on her telescope and peered closer.

"The Venture Vessel," she whispered.

What could only be the Jade Rabbit himself was now gesturing frantically, summoning her with such joyous urgency that Shabu jumped back.

"Could it be?" She looked again. And there he was.

Shabu Shabu, grand-daughter of one of the greatest adventurers of all time, resolved to travel to the Moon without delay.

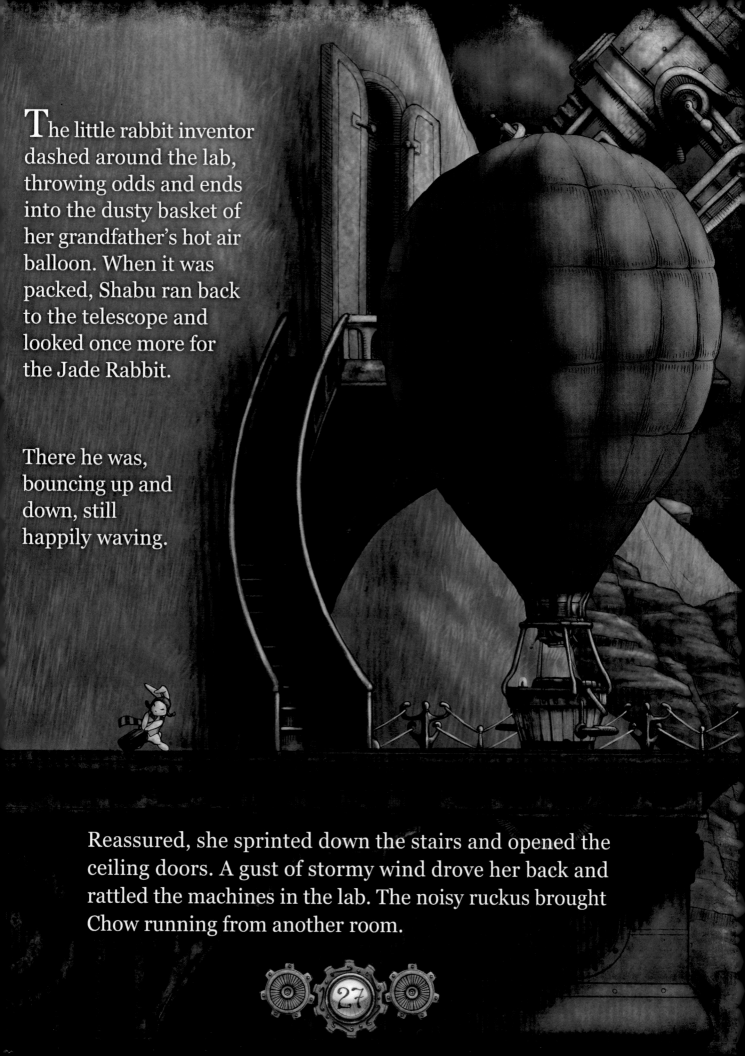

The little rabbit inventor dashed around the lab, throwing odds and ends into the dusty basket of her grandfather's hot air balloon. When it was packed, Shabu ran back to the telescope and looked once more for the Jade Rabbit.

There he was, bouncing up and down, still happily waving.

Reassured, she sprinted down the stairs and opened the ceiling doors. A gust of stormy wind drove her back and rattled the machines in the lab. The noisy ruckus brought Chow running from another room.

"**W**HAT IS ALL THAT RACKET?" hollered Chow.

"You sound just like your mother," replied Shabu as she strapped on her rucksack. "Come on, hop in!"

"Where are we going?"

"To see the Jade Rabbit, of course!"

Shabu dragged Chow to the basket and tossed him in. He had the sense to grab one of his emergency kits as he sailed over the side.

The gathering clouds had already covered the Moon and the thunder sounded closer.

"We can't fly into that storm, Shabu. It isn't safe!"

"There's no time, Chow. We have to go see him NOW!"

"But you don't believe in the Jade Rab—"

Shabu ignored him and hit the burner.

The wind grabbed the balloon and sucked it up into the storm. The terrified squirrel dug into the kit and pulled on the old parachute stuffed inside.

"He's up here, Chow, I know it!" Shabu cried as they zoomed upward in a dangerous spiral.

"Shabu! This is too dangerous! We have to get out of this storm!"

They could barely hear each other over the wind. A torrent of rain washed over them and water pooled at the bottom of the basket.

"Just a bit higher!" yelled Shabu. "We'll be safe once we're above the clouds!"

Blackness surrounded them and the wind grew still...

"KABOOM!" A bolt of lightning tore through the balloon and for a second the two friends hung motionless. Then the balloon burst into flames and the heavy basket plummeted toward the earth.

"Aaaaaah!" yelled Chow.

"Abandon ship!" yelled Shabu.

30

"Were you out of your bunny brain? What were you thinking?" Chow asked later as they dried off by the fireplace in the burrow.

"I saw him, Chow."

"Show me," said the squirrel.

Shabu led him to her telescope. The storm had finally passed and the Jade Moon shone clearly from above.

"What am I looking for again?"

"The Jade Rabbit, Noodle Head! He's there, beckoning me to join him! See him?"

"See what? There's nothing here."
Shabu shoved Chow aside and looked for herself.

"He was right there!"

Chow pulled her away and looked again. "Nope, nothing."

Shabu's nose twitched violently as she glared up at the Moon. Chow sat down on a cushion and patted the space next to him. Shabu flopped down and took a deep breath.

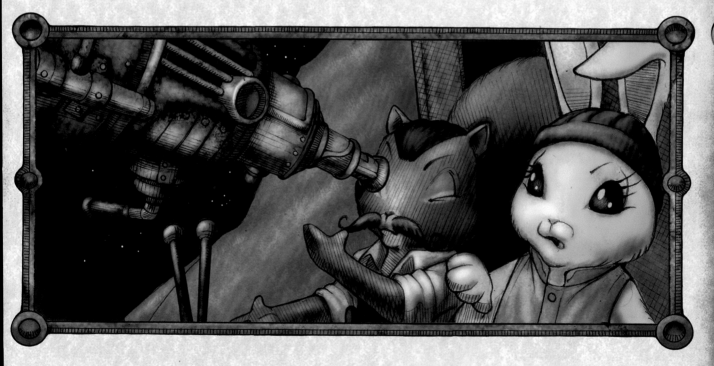

"As you know, it's the night of the Jade Moon, and I've been waiting for ages to test this new telescope—"

"Yes, Fuzzy Brain, I know. You can skip to the part where you think you saw the Jade Rabbit."

"Hey, I *did* see the Jade Rabbit!"

"Riiiiight."

"He had his own telescope, Chow! And he was looking right at me! He started jumping up and down and waving, just like this!"

Shabu leapt to her feet and did her best imitation.

"He was bright green and shiny. He had a symbol on him. It looked just like…"

Shabu froze, her eyes slightly out of focus, staring over Chow's shoulder.

"Just like what?" asked Chow.

"That's it!" Shabu grabbed the tiny brass spyglass from the desk behind Chow.

She pointed to a strange symbol.

"This is what I saw."

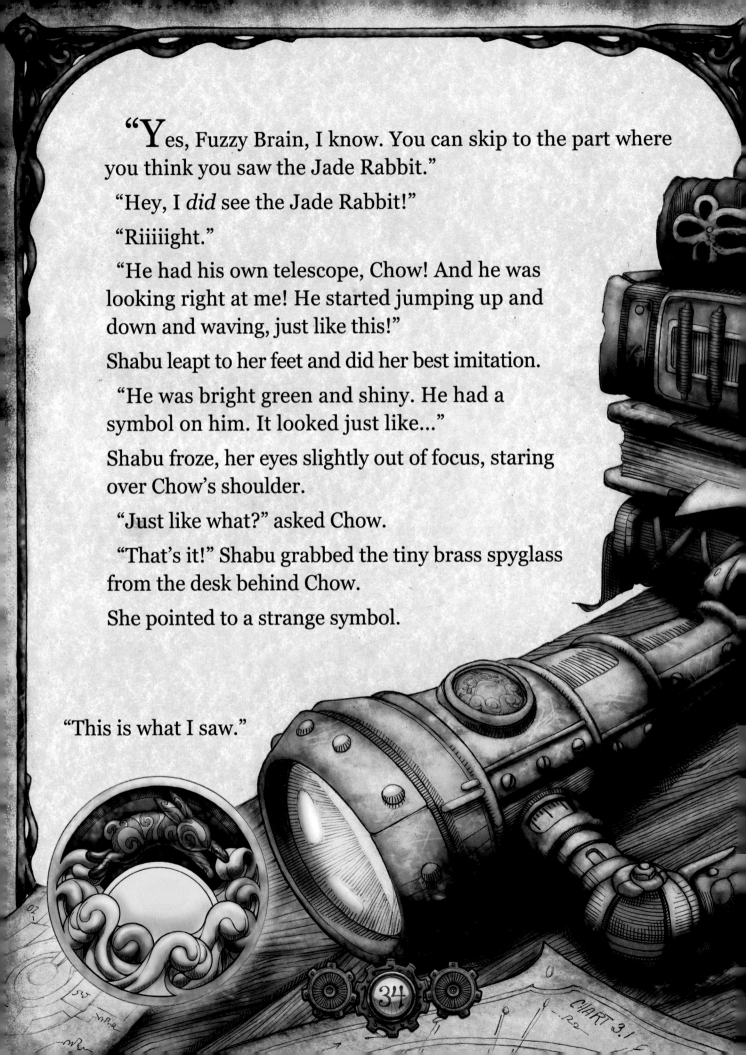

"Chow, there must be some connection between Grandfather and the Jade Rabbit. This symbol is a clue. Maybe there are more!"

Shabu and Chow combed the lab. They searched every nook and cranny, but did not find anything— no notes, drawings, diagrams or carvings resembling the symbol or the Jade Rabbit.

And no amount of gazing into the telescope brought the Jade Rabbit back into view.

Shabu dear, Don't forget the plants

Shabu swore never to give up, though Chow was finding himself quite fed up.

"Hey Noodle Head! A Messenger Mouse is here. Your mother wrote us a letter!"

My dearest Chow Chow and Shu Shu,

I hope this letter finds you both well and out of trouble now that Grandfather and I are not there to look after you. Everything is fine here, Chow. Your sister's kits are a handful, but we're managing to guide them in the right direction. It reminds me of the days when the whole family was together and you two kept us on our toes. Shabu, dear, I remember your parents so clearly before the accident. Your father used to help your grandfather in the lab while your mother tended her precious plants at the top of the stairs. I sometimes sat up there myself to write my grocery list. Well, you and Chow have each other for company though I wish I could be in two places at once. Take care of yourselves and don't forget to eat your cabbage! Write me soon.

Lovingly yours,
Mother Mien

P.S. Shabu, dear, mind you don't overfeed your mother's Cantankerous Carnivorous Hibiscus while I'm away.

"Oh, Mother's plants! I knew I was forgetting something!"

Shabu hopped up the old spiral staircase with a watering can and a jar labeled FLIES. This was her least favorite chore. Shabu wished she had inherited more of her mother's skills with plants as well as her father's and grandfather's love of inventing.

"Hey, Fuzzy Brain, have you seen my wrench?" yelled Chow from downstairs.

Shabu turned to answer. Just then, the Cantankerous Carnivorous Hibiscus stretched out a flower and snapped at her tail.

"Yeow!" yelled Shabu as the watering can fell and spilled water everywhere. Shabu marched over to the railing to give Chow a piece of her mind.

"Chow, you noodle head—" she froze. Then she saw it.

"It's been right under our noses all along!"

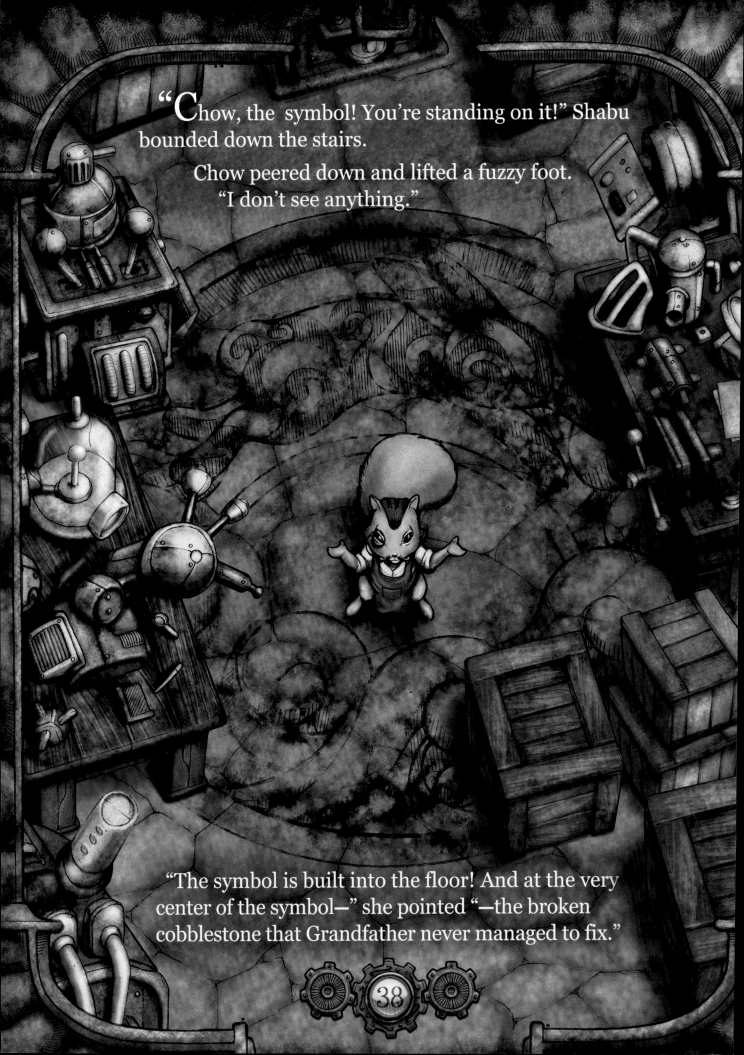

"Chow, the symbol! You're standing on it!" Shabu bounded down the stairs.

Chow peered down and lifted a fuzzy foot. "I don't see anything."

"The symbol is built into the floor! And at the very center of the symbol—" she pointed "—the broken cobblestone that Grandfather never managed to fix."

Shabu lifted the stone to reveal a small latch. She gave it a tug. Unseen gears groaned under their feet as a spiral staircase dropped from the floor and descended into darkness. The two friends looked at each other and grinned.

Each grabbed a lantern, and down the stairs they raced into the murky tunnel below.

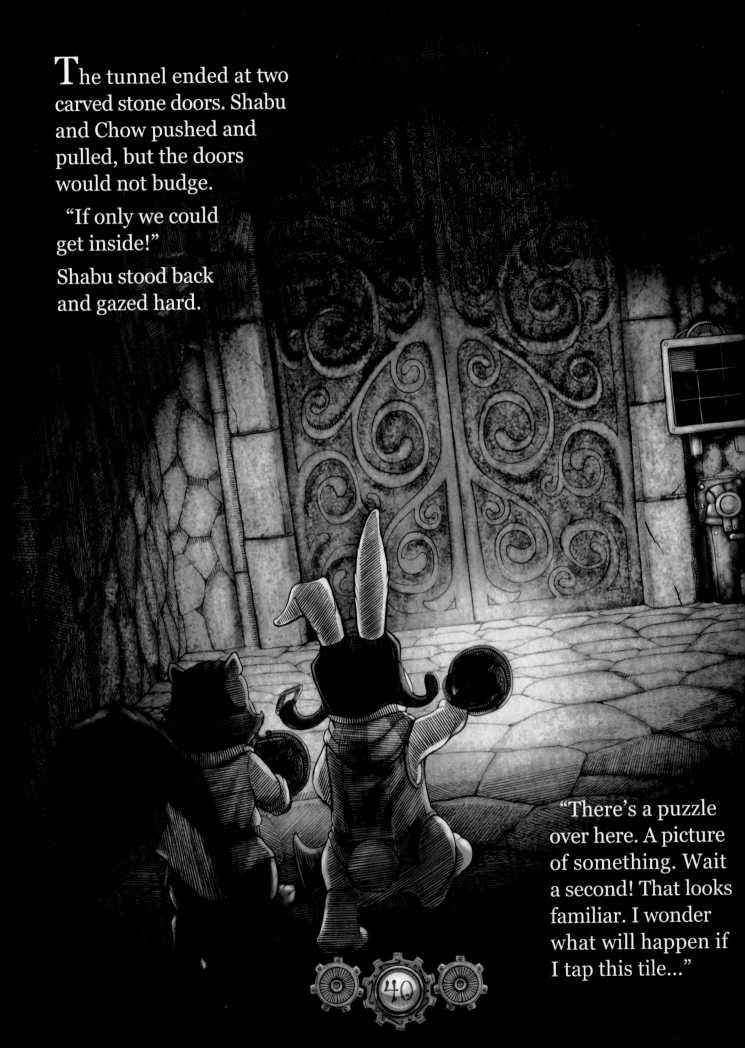

The tunnel ended at two carved stone doors. Shabu and Chow pushed and pulled, but the doors would not budge.

"If only we could get inside!"

Shabu stood back and gazed hard.

"There's a puzzle over here. A picture of something. Wait a second! That looks familiar. I wonder what will happen if I tap this tile..."

40

The tiles moved at the touch of Shabu's paw.

Her heart pounding rapidly, she worked quickly to move the final pieces into place.

With a loud groan, the huge, stone doors swung open.

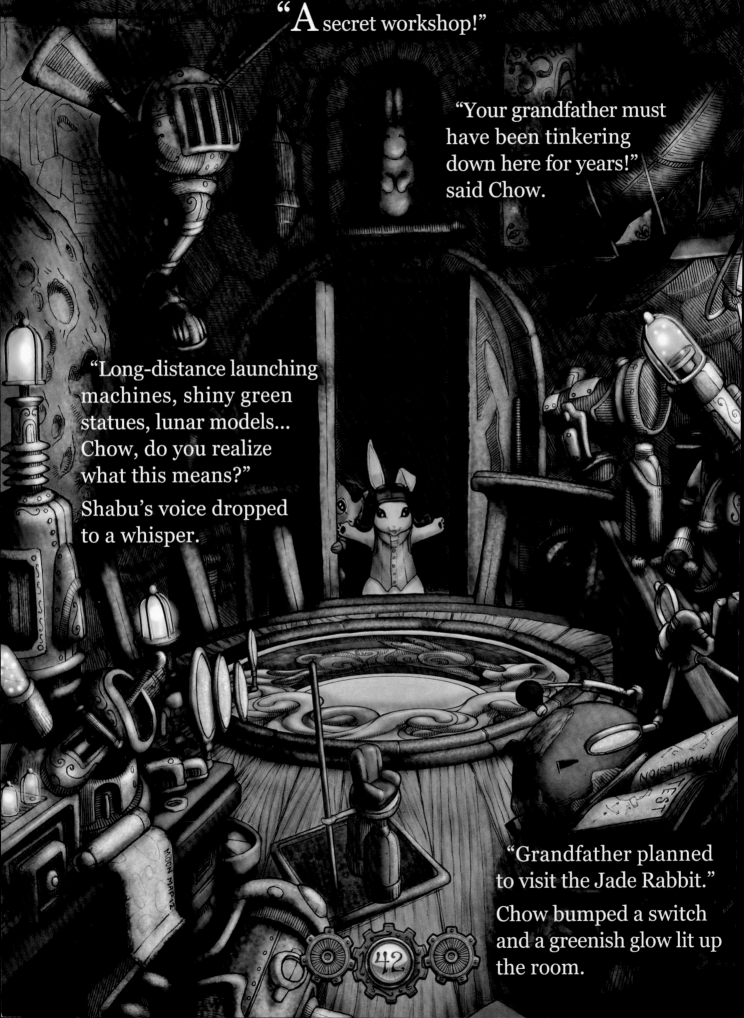

"A secret workshop!"

"Your grandfather must have been tinkering down here for years!" said Chow.

"Long-distance launching machines, shiny green statues, lunar models... Chow, do you realize what this means?"

Shabu's voice dropped to a whisper.

"Grandfather planned to visit the Jade Rabbit."

Chow bumped a switch and a greenish glow lit up the room.

42

Shabu's eyes shone. "A chance for adventure has finally blown my way, Chow. I hope you found your wrench!"

"What? No, not again! Shabu you're not suggesting—"

"That's right! First we build a new vessel,
and then we fly to the Moon!"

Thus concludes
Book 1

Join Shabu Shabu on her journey
to the Moon with

Book 2
The Silk Route

where one may or may not find the
answers to these questions:

- ✎ How does one build a ship to
  fly to the Moon?

- ✎ Will Chow find his wrench?

- ✎ Will Shabu Shabu ever water
  the plants again?

*To be
continued...*

❧ Credits ❧
Creators

Kristina Thornton
Words

Michael Csokas
Words/Pictures

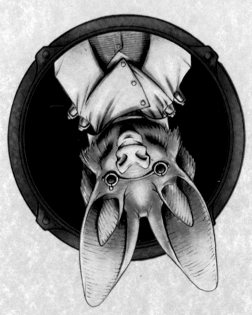

Ricardo Contreras
Color

Ola Olaniyi
Commerce

Title design by
Michelle McBri

Books so far in the **The Wee Adventures of Shabu Shabu**
eight part series:

Book 1 The Jade legend

Book 2 The Silk Route

Book 3 The Haunted Castle
Coming soon